W9-ASR-801

c. 2

STORIES FROM CENTRAL AMERICA / CUENTOS DE CENTROAMÉRICA

THE INVISIBLE HUNTERS
LOS CAZADORES INVISIBLES

A Legend from the Miskito Indians of Nicaragua
Una Leyenda de los Indios Miskitos de Nicaragua

Harriet Rohmer · Octavio Chow · Morris Vidaure
Illustrations / Ilustraciones — Joe Sam
Version in Spanish / Versión en español — Rosalma Zubizarreta & Alma Flor Ada

Art/Production Consultant: Robin Cherin
Design: Naomi Schiff, Seventeenth Street Studios
Photography: Joe Samberg

Printed in the U.S.A.

Library of Congress Cataloging-in-Publication Data
Rohmer, Harriet
      The invisible hunters.
      (Stories from Central America = Cuentos de Centroamérica)
      English and Spanish
      Summary: This Miskito Indian legend set in seventeenth-century
Nicaragua illustrates the impact of the first European traders on traditional life.
      1. Mosquito Indians—Legends.   2. Indians of Central America—
Nicaragua—Legends.   [1. Mosquito Indians—Legends.   2. Indians of Central
America—Nicaragua—Legends.   3. Spanish language materials—
Bilingual]   I. Chow, Octavio.   II. Vidaure, Morris   III. Sam, Joe, ill.   IV. Title.
V. Title: Cazadores invisibles.   VI. Series: Stories from Central America

F1529.M9R64   1987   398.2'08998   86-32658
ISBN 0-89239-031-X

The first brother grabbed the vine. Instantly, he disappeared. Then the second brother grabbed the vine and he disappeared.

The third brother cried out in fear, "What have you done with my brothers?"

"I have not harmed your brothers," answered the voice. "When they let go of me, you will see them."

The first two brothers let go of the vine. Instantly they became visible again.

"Who are you?" demanded the brothers in amazement.

"I am the Dar," said the voice. "When you hold me, neither human nor animal can see you."

El primer hermano agarró el bejuco. E instantáneamente desapareció. Entonces el segundo hermano agarró el bejuco. Y él también desapareció.

El tercer hermano, lleno de miedo, gritó:

—¿Qué les has hecho a mis hermanos?

—No les he hecho nada a tus hermanos —contestó la voz—. Cuando ellos me suelten, los verás.

Los dos primeros hermanos soltaron el bejuco. E instantáneamente se volvieron visibles.

—¿Quién eres? —preguntaron los hermanos, sorprendidos.

—Soy el Dar —dijo la voz—. Si alguien me agarra, se vuelve invisible y ni los seres humanos ni los animales lo pueden ver.

The brothers quickly understood how the Dar could help them.

"We could sneak up on the wari and they wouldn't see us."

"Then we could kill them easily with our sticks."

Each of the brothers wanted a piece of the Dar. They grabbed for it, but the vine swung away from them and disappeared.

"Before you take my power, you must promise to use it well," said the Dar.

"We will promise anything," said the brothers.

"First, you must promise never to sell the wari meat. You must give it away. Then, you must promise never to hunt with guns. You must hunt only with sticks."

Los hermanos se dieron cuenta inmediatamente de que el Dar les podía ser muy útil.

—Podríamos acercarnos a los waris sin que nos vieran.

—Luego podríamos matarlos fácilmente con nuestros palos.

Cada uno de los hermanos quería un pedazo del Dar. Se lanzaron a coger el bejuco, pero el Dar se alejó y desapareció.

—Antes de apoderarse de mi poder, tienen que prometer que lo usarán bien —dijo el Dar.

—Te prometeremos cualquier cosa —dijeron los hermanos.

—Primero tienen que prometerme que nunca venderán la carne de wari. Solamente la regalarán. Luego, tienen que prometerme que nunca cazarán con escopetas. Tienen que cazar solamente con palos.

The brothers had never sold wari meat. They had always given it to the people. They had never hunted with guns. They had always hunted with sticks. They knew no other way.

"We promise," they said. So the Dar allowed each one of them to take away a small piece of the magic vine.

That day, the brothers had great success in the hunt. After killing many wari, they hung their pieces of the Dar on the tree and started for home.

Los hermanos nunca habían vendido la carne de wari. Siempre se la habían dado a la gente. Nunca habían cazado con escopetas. Siempre habían cazado con palos. No lo sabían hacer de otra manera.

—Lo prometemos —dijeron. Y el Dar permitió que cada uno se llevase un pedazo pequeño del bejuco mágico.

Ese día los hermanos cazaron muchísimo. Después de matar muchos waris colgaron sus pedazos del Dar en el árbol y regresaron a casa.

The people of Ulwas welcomed the brothers with much rejoicing. They cleaned the animals and hung them above the fire. Soon, the delicious smell of smoking meat reached every house in the village. When the meat was ready, the brothers cut it in pieces and shared it with everyone. Never had the people of Ulwas eaten so well.

Later that night, the elders of the village asked the brothers how they had killed so many wari. The brothers told them about their promises to the Dar.

"This is truly good fortune," said the elders. "We have heard of this vine. It is very old and powerful. As long as you keep your promises, our village will prosper and our people will honor you."

La gente de Ulwas recibió a los hermanos con mucho regocijo. Limpiaron los animales y los colgaron sobre el fuego. Pronto el delicioso aroma de la carne asada llegó a todas las casas de la aldea. Cuando la carne estuvo lista, los hermanos la cortaron en pedazos y la compartieron con todos. Nunca había comido tan bien la gente de Ulwas.

Más tarde, esa noche, los ancianos de la aldea les preguntaron a los hermanos cómo habían conseguido tantos waris. Los hermanos les contaron las promesas que habían hecho al Dar.

—¡Qué buena suerte han tenido! —dijeron los ancianos—. Hemos oído hablar de ese bejuco. Es muy viejo y muy poderoso. Mientras cumplan sus promesas, nuestra aldea prosperará y nuestra gente los honrará.

With the help of the Dar, the brothers became famous hunters. Stories about them spread to all the villages along the Coco River and even beyond.

One day, a boat carrying two strangers arrived at Ulwas. The strangers greeted the brothers and gave them presents—bright-colored cloth and barrels of wine.

"We have traveled many days to meet such great hunters," they said.

The brothers invited the men to eat with them. After they had eaten, the strangers told the brothers that they were traders. They had come to buy wari meat.

"We cannot sell the wari," said the brothers, remembering their promise to the Dar. "That is what our people eat."

Con la ayuda del Dar, los hermanos se convirtieron en cazadores famosos. Se contaban cuentos sobre ellos en todas las aldeas a lo largo del Río Coco y hasta más allá.

Un día, llegó a Ulwas un barco con dos extranjeros. Los extranjeros saludaron a los hermanos y les dieron regalos: telas de muchos colores y barriles de vino.

—Hemos viajado por muchos días para conocer a estos cazadores famosos —dijeron.

Los hermanos los invitaron a comer con ellos. Después de la comida, los extranjeros les contaron a los hermanos que eran comerciantes. Habían venido a comprar carne de wari.

—No podemos vender el wari —dijeron los hermanos, acordándose de su promesa al Dar—. Eso es lo que come nuestra gente.

The traders laughed. "We never expected that such great hunters would be so foolish. Of course your people have to eat. We only want to buy what they don't eat."

The brothers were tempted. "Maybe we could sell just a little meat," said the first brother.

"But the Dar will know," said the second brother.

The brothers looked at each other nervously. Then the third brother said, "We have seen that the traders are clever men. Their power must be greater than the power of the Dar."

The brothers nodded. It would not be wise to displease the traders.

So the brothers began to sell the wari.

Los comerciantes se rieron. —Nunca pensamos que cazadores tan famosos fueran tan tontos. Claro que la gente tiene que comer. Solamente queremos comprar lo que sobra.

Los hermanos se sintieron tentados. Hablaron entre sí. —Quizás pudiéramos vender nada más un poco de carne —dijo el primer hermano.

—Pero el Dar lo sabrá —dijo el segundo hermano.

Los hermanos se miraron nerviosamente. Entonces el tercer hermano dijo.

—Hemos visto que los comerciantes son hombres muy hábiles. Su poder tiene que ser mayor que el poder del Dar.

Los otros hermanos asintieron. No valdría la pena disgustar a los comerciantes.

Así que los hermanos comenzaron a vender la carne de wari.

The traders returned many times to the village of
Ulwas. Each time they brought more money for the hunters.
Each time they took away more wari. Soon the brothers were
worried that there was not enough wari for the people.

Los comerciantes regresaron varias veces al pueblo de
Ulwas. Cada vez traían más dinero para los cazadores. Cada vez
se llevaban más wari. Pronto los hermanos empezaron a preocu-
parse al ver que no había suficiente wari para el pueblo.

The traders laughed at their worries. "It is your own fault for hunting with sticks," they said.

"But we have always hunted with sticks."

"That is why you cannot feed your people. You need to kill the wari faster. You need guns."

The brothers talked things over. "If we bought guns, we could kill more wari," said the first brother. "We could sell to the traders and feed the people too."

"But what will happen to us?" asked the second brother.

The third brother laughed before he answered. "We will become clever men—like the traders."

So the brothers began to hunt with guns. They had completely forgotten their promise to the Dar.

Los comerciantes se rieron de sus preocupaciones.
—Es culpa de ustedes por cazar solamente con palos —dijeron.

—Pero siempre hemos cazado con palos.

—Ésa es la razón por la que no pueden alimentar a su pueblo. Tienen que cazar los waris más rápidamente. Necesitan escopetas.

Los hermanos conversaron entre sí.

—Si compráramos escopetas, podríamos cazar más waris —dijo el primer hermano—. Podríamos vender a los comerciantes y alimentar al pueblo también.

—Pero, ¿qué nos pasará? —preguntó el segundo hermano.

El tercer hermano se rió antes de contestar. —Nos convertiremos en hombres hábiles como los comerciantes.

Así que los hermanos comenzaron a cazar con escopetas. Se olvidaron por completo de su promesa al Dar.

Little by little their hearts turned away from the people. The more meat they brought home, the more they sold to the traders. They were becoming accustomed to the things that money could buy.

The elders of the village spoke sternly to the brothers. "You must feed the people. They are hungry."

The brothers answered angrily, "If they want meat, they can pay us for it like the traders do!"

Poco a poco, sus corazones se alejaron de su gente. Mientras más carne cazaban, más vendían a los comerciantes. Se estaban acostumbrando a las cosas que podían comprar con el dinero que ganaban.

Los ancianos del pueblo hablaron seriamente a los hermanos.

—Necesitan darle de comer a la gente. Tienen hambre.

Los hermanos respondieron, enojados. —¡Si quieren comer carne, nos pueden pagar por ella como hacen los comerciantes!

But the people had no money. They began to wait for the hunters outside the village. When the hunters returned loaded down with wari, the people demanded meat.

"Clever men do not give away what they can sell," said the hunters to each other. So they gave the people spoiled meat, which they could not sell.

The people were angry. "Are you no longer our brothers?" they shouted.

The hunters laughed and went on their way. They even pushed aside the elders who tried to reason with them.

Pero la gente no tenía dinero. Comenzaron a esperar a los cazadores en las afueras del pueblo. Cuando los cazadores regresaban cargados de wari, la gente les pedía carne.

—Los hombres listos no regalan lo que pueden vender —se dijeron los cazadores. Así que les daban a la gente la carne malograda que no se podía vender.

La gente se enojó. —¿Ya no son ustedes nuestros hermanos? —les gritaron.

Los cazadores se reían y seguían su camino. Hasta hicieron a un lado a los ancianos que trataban de razonar con ellos.

Many months passed. One day when the brothers returned to the village, the people did not crowd around them as usual. Instead, they backed away. Some covered their eyes and screamed. Others stared in disbelief at the strange procession of dead wari moving slowly through the air. Only the elders understood what had happened.

"The Dar has made the hunters invisible," they said.

It was true. The brothers were invisible. They had left their pieces of Dar at the tree as they always did, but they were still invisible. Something had gone wrong.

They dropped the animals they were carrying and raced through the bush to the tree.

Así pasaron muchos meses. Un día, cuando los hermanos regresaron al pueblo, la gente no se reunió a su alrededor como de costumbre. Algunos se cubrieron los ojos y gritaron. Otros miraron incrédulos a la extraña procesión de waris muertos que se movía lentamente por el aire. Sólo los ancianos entendieron qué era lo que pasaba.

—El Dar ha vuelto invisibles a los cazadores — dijeron.

Era verdad. Los hermanos eran invisibles. Habían dejado sus pedazos de Dar en el árbol como de costumbre, pero habían permanecido invisibles. Algo no iba bien.

Soltaron los animales que llevaban y corrieron hasta el árbol.

"What have you done?" they asked the Dar in terror.
But the Dar did not answer them.
The brothers fell to their knees and begged for help.
But the Dar only repeated its name over and over.
"Dar. Dar. Dar."
Then the brothers realized what terrible things they had done, and they were ashamed. Tearfully, they made their way home.

—¿Qué nos has hecho? —le preguntaron alarmados al Dar.

Pero el Dar no les contestó.

Los hermanos cayeron de rodillas y le rogaron al Dar que les ayudara.

Pero el Dar sólo repitió su nombre una y otra vez.

—Dar. Dar. Dar.

Entonces los hermanos se dieron cuenta de las cosas terribles que habían hecho y se sintieron muy avergonzados. Llorando, regresaron a su casa.

Outside the village the elders were waiting. The brothers pleaded for forgiveness, but the elders did not forgive them.

"From this moment on, you are banished from Ulwas," they said. "Never again will you live with us."

The brothers begged the elders for one more chance. "How can we live away from our people?" they cried.

But the elders turned their backs on them and walked away.

So the invisible hunters left their village forever. They wandered up the Coco River as far as the falls at Carizal. As they wandered, they called out to the Dar, begging to become visible again.

En las afueras del pueblo los esperaban los ancianos. Los hermanos les rogaron que los perdonaran, pero los ancianos no los perdonaron.

—Desde este momento, tienen que irse de Ulwas— dijeron—. Nunca más vivirán con nosotros.

Los hermanos les rogaron a los ancianos que les dieran una última oportunidad. —¿Cómo podemos vivir lejos de nuestra gente? —dijeron llorando.

Pero los ancianos les dieron la espalda y se fueron.

Así que los cazadores invisibles dejaron su pueblo para siempre. Deambularon por las márgenes del río Coco y llegaron hasta las cataratas de Carizal. Mientras vagaban, llamaban al Dar, rogándole que los volviera visibles de nuevo.

Some of the Miskito people from the Coco River say that the hunters are still wandering after all these years. A few even say that the invisible hunters have passed them in the bush. They know it is true, they say, because they have heard voices calling, "Dar. Dar. Dar."

Algunos de los miskitos del río Coco dicen que los cazadores todavía vagan después de todos estos años. Algunos hasta dicen que los cazadores invisibles han pasado junto a ellos en el monte. Saben que es así, dicen, porque han oído voces que llaman: —Dar. Dar. Dar.

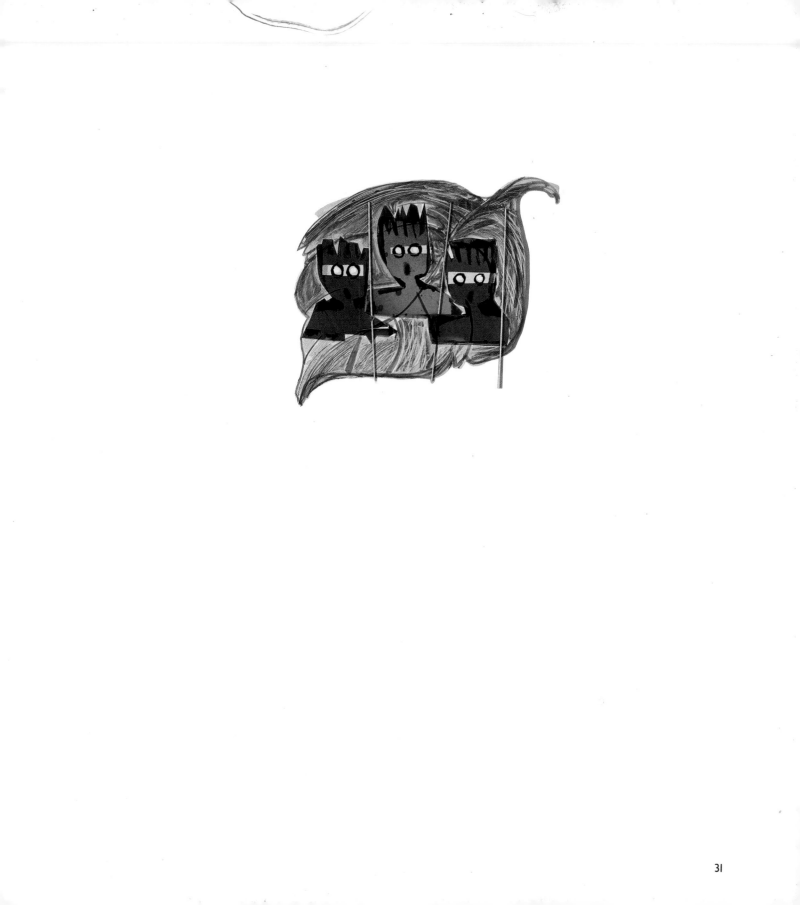

ABOUT THE STORY

The legend of *The Invisible Hunters* documents the first moments of contact between an indigenous culture and the outside world. While this story takes place in the Miskito Indian village of Ulwas in northern Nicaragua, it is also a metaphor for what has happened to traditional cultures in many other parts of the world.

The story came to me in fragments. My research into the anthropological archives turned up references to a wandering band of invisible Miskito hunters. I asked about them on my first visit to the Atlantic Coast of Nicaragua in 1983, but without success. Fortunately, my quest came to the attention of Father Agustín Sambola, an Afro-Indian Catholic priest who was greatly respected by the Miskitos in the north. He invited me to accompany him on a visit to the outlying Miskito communities of his parish.

As I was about to join Agustín in January, 1984, word came that his jeep had been ambushed by "contra" mercenaries who were trying to overthrow the Nicaraguan government. Miraculously, Agustín was unhurt. The journey went off as planned; and in the mining town of La Rosita, I met Octavio Chow, an elder Miskito Catholic deacon who knew of the story and added to it. Speaking in Miskito which his son Martín translated into Spanish, Octavio told me about the magic Dar vine which gives whoever holds it the power of invisibility.

Was there someone who could tell me more of the story? On my return to the capital city of Managua, Bishop John Wilson of the Protestant Moravian Church, himself part Miskito, arranged for a meeting with lay pastor Morris Vidaure. Morris had grown up in a Miskito village on the Atlantic Coast and was a leader in his community. "According to the stories I heard as a child," he told me, "the Dar has a voice. I can take you to people who say they have heard that voice."

More than three years have passed since I began to put together this tale. I hope it will fascinate you as it has fascinated me. More than that, I hope that the young North Americans who read this story will gain a new understanding and respect for the people of Central America. For without understanding and respect there can be no hope for peace with dignity in our hemisphere.

San Francisco artist Joe Sam was born in Harlem, New York. Now a major California artist, he is known for his powerful portrayals of Afro-American life. This is his first picture book for young people.

My thanks go to Father Agustín Sambola, Bishop John Wilson, Rev. Norman Bent, Ray Hooker, Sixto Ulloa, Martín Chow, David Schecter, Alicia Muñoz, Roxanne Dunbar Ortiz, Norma Smith, Larry Yep, Joanne Ryder and to the many people of the Atlantic Coast of Nicaragua who offered their help and inspiration.

Harriet Rohmer
San Francisco, California
December, 1986

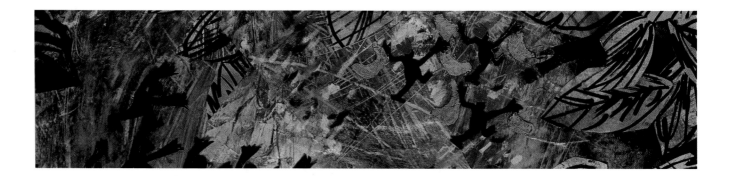